THE MYSTERY OF THE DANCING SHOES

AND OTHER ROMANIAN FAIRY TALES

PETRE ISPIRESCU

Translated by

ALEXA J ISPAS

ISBN: 978-1-913926-11-3 (ebk)

ISBN: 978-1-913926-14-4 (pbk)

CONTENTS

lator's Note in which I summarize the changes I have made, for any readers who would like to know more about how my translated and adapted version differs from the original.

I have also used that section to add short pieces of personal commentary focused on various aspects of the story, as well as to point readers to related tales or other relevant resources that may be of interest.

This type of direct message from the translator to the reader is rather unusual in translated works, but I hope that readers will enjoy the transparency and added insight these sections provide.

As such, the books in the *Romanian Stories* series also represent an experiment in the art of putting together a translated version of a piece of work.

If you enjoy these stories, you can find more at www.storybothy.com

THE MYSTERY OF THE DANCING SHOES

There was once a poor young orphan lad who worked as a servant to make ends meet.

He was so clever and skilled that all the village boys were envious of him.

They kept making fun of him so he would feel bad about himself and seek out their company, but he didn't care about their chatter and was minding his own business.

When they would gather up in the evenings to gossip, he pretended he didn't understand their jokes.

His masters, on the other hand, were very happy with him.

He was also favored by the village girls, who would nudge each other and look at him from underneath their eyebrows whenever they saw him.

And they indeed had something to look at.

He was handsome, with dark locks fluttering in the wind and framing his cheeks white as snow.

His little moustache was barely sprouting, as if it was a shadow on his upper lip.

And the eyes? His eyes were breaking all the girls' hearts.

When he was taking the cows to pasture, the girls kept trying to chat him up.

They had nicknamed him the Prince Charming of the village.

But he ignored them and pretended he didn't understand what they wanted.

In addition to being good-looking, everything he laid his hands on came out well.

The cows he was taking to pasture were healthier than those that were looked after by the other servants.

They gave more milk than other cows, because he took them places where the grass tasted better and gave more nourishment.

Wherever he walked you could tell, because even the grass was rejoicing.

It turns out that he had been born at a good moment and it had been prophesized that he had a bright future ahead of him.

But he had no inkling about this and didn't know what his future held.

Instead, he was humble and kept minding his own business.

He did not take issue with anyone's words or interfere with other people's belongings.

And for this very thing, the other lads and servants were envious of him.

One spring day, tired from having walked all over the place with the cows, he lay down under the shadow of a large tree and went to sleep.

He had already chosen that spot for such an eventuality.

The tree under which he slept was located in a valley decorated with all sorts of little flowers, all in bloom.

Somewhat further along there was a little stream, which originated from the sides of a small hill.

The stream was meandering through bushes and other weeds through which it had carved its path, and the gurgling of the water seemed to invite you to sleep.

The tree under which he had fallen asleep was so tall and majestic, it seemed to touch the sky.

Little birds were nuzzling one another and building nests through its branches.

Listening to their song would be enough to light the fire of love in anyone's heart.

As soon as he put his head down in that spot, he fell asleep.

He dreamt that he saw a beautiful fairy who told him to go to the court of the local king to seek his fortune.

When he woke up, he wondered about the meaning of that dream.

He wrestled with his thoughts all day long, but couldn't find any clarity.

He didn't know that the star under which he had been born had come to serve him.

The next day, while taking the cows to pasture, he made a detour by the tree under which he had slept the day before.

He once again fell asleep by its root, and dreamt the same dream.

He was even more confused than the first time, and spent the rest of the day wrestling with his thoughts.

On the third day went to the same tree, slept in the same spot, and had the same dream for the third time in a row.

This time, the fairy threatened him with illness and all sorts of human evils if he doesn't go.

He decided to do as the fairy had told him to do, and see what happens.

He returned home with the cows, took them into the stable, then asked to see his master.

"Master," he said, "I have decided to go out into the world and seek my fortune. I have been a servant for a long time, and I don't see this changing any time soon unless I make different life choices. I would like you to give me my dues."

"But why are you leaving my service, lad?" his master said. "Are you not happy with the wages I am paying you? Do you not have enough food? Better stay with me, boy, and I will find you a good girl from the village, with a little dowry. I will also help you out as much as my heart will let me, so you find your place here like all the other villagers. Don't go off wandering into the world and risk becoming homeless and poor."

"I am happy in your service, master. I have enough food and everything else I need, but I simply feel the need to go out into the world, and I have made up my mind."

When his master saw that there was no way to keep him there, he gave him the little he was due, and the boy set off into the world.

As soon as he left the village, the lad went to the royal court, where he got hired to work in the king's garden.

The gardener was delighted to take him on when he saw him so handsome and well-mannered.

He had previously received complaints from the king's daughters, who said that he kept hiring the ugliest and most disgusting young lads to be found on this earth.

As handsome as the boy was, the clothes he had were of poor quality.

The gardener gave him new clothes of good quality, fit for a royal gardener's helper.

And as he was handsome, the clothes suited him well.

Aside from the gardening, he was tasked with putting together twelve small bunches of flowers every day.

He would deliver these bunches of flowers to

the twelve princesses when they walked through the garden each morning.

It had been prophesized that these princesses would not be able to marry until someone would break the curse that had been placed upon them and make one of them fall in love.

As part of the curse, the Fates had made them addicted to dancing.

Every night, the girls would dance so much that they would break one pair of dancing shoes made of white satin.

Yet nobody could figure out where they went to dance.

The king had become worried about their icy heart, which wouldn't warm to any of the young suitors who had come to ask for their hand in marriage.

Besides, he was sick and tired of spending so much money on new dancing shoes every day.

He sent out a message throughout his country and countries further afield that if any young man can tell him how his daughters manage to escape the palace and destroy a pair of dancing shoes every night, he can choose one of the princesses as his wife.

The king kept all his daughters in the same

room in his palace, behind nine iron doors locked by nine large locks.

Yet nobody knew what they did to destroy their shoes, as nobody had seen them leave the palace at night.

It turns out that unless anyone succeeded in breaking the curse, this is how the princesses were destined to spend the rest of their lives.

As soon as news of the king's offer spread, suitors started pouring in.

Some were sons of rulers and kings, others sons of aristocrats, some even sons of less prominent aristocrats.

Each of these suitors was tasked with standing guard at the princesses' door for one night.

The king was waiting with great trepidation each morning for someone to bring him good news.

But instead, by the morning, the young lads who had stood guard could no longer be found.

Nobody knew what had happened to them. There was not even a single trace left of them.

Eleven young lads had so far disappeared, and this had given the other suitors pause for thought, as they realized the danger they were putting themselves in by offering to stand guard.

And so, one by one, they left the king's court and returned to their homes, leaving the king's daughters in God's care.

Nobody wanted to lose their soul for a pretty face.

The king was in shock.

How had the young men vanished?

He no longer dared invite anyone to try his luck, and started to worry that his daughters would grow into old spinsters.

Meanwhile, the boy was fulfilling his job as a garden servant as best he could.

The princesses were happy with the bunches of flowers he was giving them every morning, and the gardener was happy with his work.

When the young lad was giving the bunches of flowers to the young ladies, he did not dare lift his eyes towards them, except for the youngest daughter.

When it was her turn to receive the flowers, he didn't know why, but he kept blushing, and his heart was racing so hard it felt as if it might jump out of his chest.

The girl noticed this, but thought that the

young lad is shy and that is why he blushes while standing before her.

This happened day after day, and he began to worry about having his heart broken.

He knew that due to his low status as a garden servant, he could not hope to attract the attention of a beautiful princess, especially one who seemed so distant and ice-cold towards him.

Yet he could not stop his heart from going wild every time he came close to her.

He would have liked to try his luck and stand guard, but he had heard of what had happened to those who had made the attempt before him.

One day, the youngest daughter confided in her sisters that she thought the servant who was giving them the flowers every morning was rather handsome.

As soon as the eldest daughter heard such words come out of her youngest sisters' mouth, she started making fun of her.

How could she utter such nice words about a servant?

Had she started giving away her heart to him?

Meanwhile, the boy's heart was telling him to

go before the king and ask to stand guard, but he knew his place.

He was too scared to lose his job and be left with nothing.

Also, he hadn't forgotten what had happened to the lads who had vanished.

Then there was the thought that troubled him most.

If he were to be thrown out of the royal court, he wouldn't see the king's youngest daughter again.

While giving her flowers every morning, however much he tried to temper his passion, he felt irresistibly attracted to her.

No longer being able to touch her fingers ever morning would be unbearable.

Day and night, he was wrestling with these thoughts and didn't know what to do about them.

One night, as he fell asleep thinking about the king's youngest daughter, he once again dreamt of the fairy.

"Go into the corner of the garden the furthest towards the East," the fairy said. "There you will find two laurel tree seedlings, one of cherry color and the other of rose color. Next to them you will see a golden shovel, a golden watering can, and a silk towel. Take these seedlings and put them in two beautiful flower pots. Dig them with the golden shovel, water them with the golden watering can, and wipe them gently with the silk towel. Take care of them like the light in your eyes. Once they are fully grown, you will be able to ask them to fulfill any wish you have."

After saying this, she vanished like a ghost, and the gardener's servant didn't even have time to thank her.

He shook off his sleep and ran to the corner of the garden closest to the East.

He was overjoyed when he found the things exactly as the fairy had told him.

He wiped his eyes and pinched himself to make sure he wasn't still dreaming.

After he reassured himself that he was awake, he took the laurel tree seedlings.

He took care of them as the fairy had taught him, regularly digging them with the golden shovel, watering them with the golden watering can, and wiping them with the silk towel.

The laurel trees were growing and getting stronger as if by miracle.

Not long passed and they became fully

grown laurel trees, more beautiful than anyone had ever seen.

One day, he went to them and spoke as the fairy had taught him.

"Laurel tree, laurel tree," he said, "I have dug you with the golden shovel, I have watered you with the golden watering can, and I have wiped you with the silk towel. Give me the gift of becoming unseen by anybody whenever I want."

He was surprised when at that very moment, he saw a flower bud appearing and growing before his eyes.

Within instants, the flower bud became a flower so beautiful, you felt compelled to take in its perfume.

He gently took hold of the flower, plucked it, and put it close to his chest.

As soon as he did this, he saw his lower body become invisible, and felt certain that his upper body had become invisible too.

In the evening, when the princesses went into their bedroom, he snuck past them without any of them seeing him.

Then he waited to see what the girls would do.

Instead of getting ready for bed, they started

combing their hair and putting on expensive clothes.

It was obvious they were preparing to go somewhere, so he decided to follow them, to see where they went.

Suddenly, the eldest said:

"Are you ready, sisters?"

"We're ready," the others said.

Then the eldest tapped her foot and a trap door appeared.

The girls, followed by the lad, lowered themselves through it and kept going down until they reached a garden surrounded by a wall made of copper.

When they were about to enter, the eldest girl again tapped her foot and the steel gates of the garden opened.

As he followed the girls into the garden, the lad stepped on the youngest girl's dress by mistake.

The girl, turning quickly, didn't see anyone, but she remained suspicious.

"Sisters, I am thinking someone may have followed me," she told her sisters. "I felt someone stepping on my dress."

Her sisters looked everywhere but couldn't see anyone.

"Don't be silly," they said. "Who could have followed us without us noticing? Your dress probably got caught in some thorns."

The girl didn't say anything, but it was obvious she was still on her guard.

The lad kept following them.

They passed through a forest with silver leaves, through another forest with golden leaves, and another one with leaves made entirely of diamonds and other precious stones.

The stones were shining so brightly they would make you blind.

Eventually, they reached a large lake.

In the middle of the lake was a little hill and on top of this hill were some palaces, more beautiful than anyone could imagine.

The king's palaces were nothing compared to these, which shone brighter than the sun.

They were so ingeniously crafted that when you went up inside them you thought you were going down, and when you were going down you thought you were going up.

Twelve tiny boats with rowers clothed

entirely in gold were waiting at the edge of the lake.

Each of the girls climbed into one of the boats, while the boy climbed into the youngest girl's boat.

The boats were going in a line, each boat at an equal distance from the boat in front of it, but the youngest girl's boat soon started lagging behind.

The rower was working as hard as he could to keep up with the others.

He kept wondering why his boat was lagging behind despite him putting in far more effort than on all the previous nights.

As soon as they reached the other side of the pond, music started playing in the distance.

It was the kind of music that made you want to dance and immerse yourself in its rhythm.

The girls jumped out of the boats as fast as lightning, went inside the palace, and started to dance with some young lads.

It turns out these were the young lads who had stood guard by their bedroom door and had vanished without trace.

The boy kept following them and watched as

the girls danced and started wearing out their shoes.

The ballroom, which was decorated with gold and precious stones, was so large you could barely see where it ended.

There were torches all around, as big as a person, that were burning like liquid gold.

The walls were as white as milk and were shining brighter than the sun.

They were decorated with streaks of gold, as well as rubies and other gemstones that were flickering like fire.

The boy found an observation spot in one of the corners and looked at all these marvels.

He had plenty to look at, and he danced while doing so, because there was no way to stand still while that music played.

Even the torches and the tables were jumping up and down, as if by magic.

Organs, flutes, guitars, horns, lutes, and many other instruments were playing in harmony, making the most enticing music in the entire world.

And the girls? They were dancing wildly, one dance after the other, wearing their shoes down more and more as the night went on.

They danced until daybreak, when the music suddenly stopped playing.

At that moment, a table laden with all kinds of delicious foods sprung up from the ground.

The girls and their dance partners all sat down at that table, and they ate and feasted to their heart's desire.

The boy kept his distance and watched all this from his corner of the room, even though his mouth watering.

Eventually the girls finished eating and set off home, returning the same way they had come.

The lad kept following them like a shadow.

While they were passing through the forest with silver leaves, the lad broke off a tiny branch from one of the trees.

Suddenly the entire forest started rumbling, as if a storm had descended upon the trees, yet not a single leaf was moving.

The girls jumped up.

"What is that, sisters?" the youngest one said.

"What can it be?" the eldest sister said. "Perhaps the little bird that has its nest on top of the church tower in our father's palaces has flown through the leaves, because only she can reach this place."

The girls passed through the forest and reached their father's palace.

They re-entered their bedroom using the trap door, which sealed itself shut behind them.

The next morning, when the boy assembled the bunches of flowers for the king's daughters, he hid the little branch he had broken off inside the youngest girl's bunch.

The princess was surprised when she looked through her bunch of flowers and found it.

She couldn't figure out how he could have gotten hold of that little branch.

The next evening, the girls spent the same way, and the lad used his invisibility powers again to follow them.

This time he broke off a tiny twig from the trees with golden leaves.

The eldest girl, again with soothing words, allied the fear of her sisters when the rumble went through the forest after the boy had broken off the twig.

The following morning, the lad put the twig among the flowers he gave to the youngest of the girls.

When the girl received her bunch of flowers

and found the twig hidden among them, she felt a burning iron go through her heart.

She looked out for the right opportunity and when it came, she went into the garden and pretended to go for a walk.

She found the boy upon turning a corner and took him aside, where they could not be seen.

"Where did you get that twig you put into my bunch of flowers?" she asked him.

"A place your Highness knows all too well."

"So you have followed us and know where we are going at night."

"Something like that."

"How did you manage not to be seen by any of us?"

"I hid."

"Take a bag of gold coins, and don't breathe a word about our nightly adventures."

"I am not selling my silence, your Highness."

"If I hear you have as much as dropped one word about it, I will order to have your head cut off."

Even though she uttered these harsh words, her heart was in another mood altogether.

It seemed to her that this young man was getting more handsome by the day.

The third night, when he followed them, he broke off a twig from the trees with diamond leaves.

Again the forest rumbled, and the eldest sister once again dismissed the incident as insignificant.

The youngest of the girls, however, without knowing why, felt a hidden joy creeping into her heart.

The next day, when she found the diamond twig in her bunch of flowers, she looked at the boy from underneath her eyelashes and thought that he looked more handsome than the sons of rulers and kings.

The young man snuck a peak in her direction as well, and as their eyes met, he saw her lose her icy cold look for a moment.

He pretended he didn't understand what was happening and went about his business.

Yet the eldest of the girls caught them talking and started making fun of her younger sister.

The youngest girl did not say anything and swallowed her shame.

She couldn't understand how the young man had managed to discover their secret, and she started to think that this lad had some sort of magic powers.

He seemed to know things even wizards didn't know.

And then, his majestic stance, his handsome and kind face, did not fit his low status as a servant.

On top of being handsome, he had a sort of 'come hither' look about him that attracted her.

After the girls finished their walk through the garden, the youngest of the girls told them that the garden servant knew everything they did at night.

The girls drew up a plan to make him lose his heart and his senses, as they had done with the other young lads.

But the lad guessed they were about to talk about him, so he used his invisibility powers to sneak in behind them and listen to their plans.

Once he heard everything he needed to know, he went to his laurel trees and said to the rose-colored one:

"Laurel tree, laurel tree, I have dug you with a golden shovel, have watered you with a golden watering can, and dried you with a silk towel.

Give me as much learning and money as a king's son."

As before, a flower bud sprouted, grew, and a wonderful flower blossomed right before his eyes.

He took the flower and put it close to his chest.

Immediately, the sunburns disappeared from his face, leaving it clean and light, as if he had just been born.

He also felt something going on in his brain, something he couldn't understand, but he noticed he had started thinking differently from before.

His mind had become sharper, and he also noticed that his clothes had completely transformed.

He was now wearing the kind of expensive clothes that sons of kings wore.

Then he went to the king and asked to stand guard at the girls' bedroom door that night.

The king felt sorry for his youth and advised him to go about his own business instead of seeking his own death.

But the young man insisted and in the end, the king agreed.

The king didn't even suspect this was his

garden servant, that is how much the lad had changed.

When he showed him to the girls and the king told them what he wanted, they didn't recognize him either.

Only the youngest one recognized him and started feeling love in her heart.

The following night, when they set off to their dance, they took him with them.

He knew what to expect, but didn't reveal anything about what he knew.

They reached the enchanted palace, danced until daybreak, then sat down to eat.

While they were eating, he was offered a drink.

This was the same drink that had been offered to all the young lads before him, who had mysteriously vanished and were now living inside the enchanted palace.

This drink was meant to make the person who drank it lose their mind and vanish from the daytime world.

He took the drink in his hand and looked at the youngest of the girls with tears in his eyes, full of the love that was consuming him.

"I am prepared to drink this for you," he said,

"if you want me to. But I am hoping that your heart is not so icy as to allow this to happen."

"I no longer have an icy heart," she said, "the fire of your love has thawed the ice. Don't drink. I'd rather be the wife of a gardener's servant for the rest of my life."

Everyone heard her words, and he threw the drink behind him.

At that moment, the spell broke, and the enchanted palace vanished, as if it had never existed.

They all found themselves in the king's palace.

When the king saw them, he was thunderstruck.

The lad, his former gardener's servant, told him everything he had seen while accompanying the princesses, and explained to the king the reason why his daughters had been wearing out their dancing shoes night after night.

The king allowed the youngest of the girls to marry the young handsome lad.

Then the other girls also came before him with one of the lads that had vanished and that had come back to their senses once the spell had broken.

The king was delighted that his daughters no longer had an icy heart and allowed each of them to set up their own home.

There was great rejoicing, as the many weddings were celebrated one after the other.

Before they married, the youngest girls asked her fiancé what magic he had used to discover the girls' secret.

He told her about the two laurel trees.

She decided to cut them down and turn them to ashes, so they could have a normal life together, devoid of magic spells.

Then they married and lived a happy life, the way a happy life is lived in this world of ours, until they got worn down by deep old age.

And I jumped into a saddle and told you the story thus.

TRANSLATOR'S NOTE (THE MYSTERY OF THE DANCING SHOES)

This story's original title was 'Cele Douasprezece Fete de Imparat', which translates as 'The King's Twelve Daughters'.

I have changed it to *The Mystery of the Dancing Shoes* because I wanted to highlight the mystery that is at the heart of this story.

If you are a creative person looking for inspiration, this story has so much to offer: a complex love story, an interesting character arc, an intoxicating night-time ritual.

Of all the elements of this story, I found the night-time dancing the most intriguing.

Uncontrolled dancing offers a powerful metaphor for addiction, one that is found in many other fantasy stories.

I was reminded of Hans Christian Andersen's story *The Red Shoes*, as well as the night-time dancing ritual in Susanna Clarke's novel *Jonathan Strange & Mr Norrell*.

For those in the grips of such an addiction, or for those who have loved ones in this situation, *The Mystery of the Dancing Shoes* offers a powerful healing balm.

It shows a way to break the addiction curse through the power of love.

The girl's decision to destroy the laurel trees that had provided her husband with magical help is interesting and worth mentioning.

Choosing the groundedness of reality over the intoxicating world of magic is a theme that shows up in many of the stories collected by Petre Ispirescu.

For example, you can find this theme expressed in *Youth Everlasting* (the headline story in *Youth Everlasting and Other Romanian Fairy Tales*), as well as in *The Magic Wolf*, the final story in this book.

We can only speculate about the reason for the popularity of this theme in Romanian folklore.

My interpretation is that these stories were

told by people living within the harsh realities of agrarian life.

While the magic in the stories provided them with much-needed entertainment, the ability to accept the limitations of physical reality was essential to their way of life.

By contrast, in Western more recent fantasy stories, such as *Lud-in-the-Mist* by Hope Mirrlees, or *Neverwhere* by Neil Gaiman, the characters are so enchanted by their discovery of magic that they choose to abandon their previous mundane existence.

GREUCEANU

Once upon a time, there was a king who was very upset because some *zmei*, fearsome human-like creatures with magic powers, had stolen the sun and the moon from the sky.

He therefore sent messengers through all the corners of his kingdom, to let everyone know that whichever hero will succeed in taking the sun and the moon back from the *zmei*, that hero will receive half his kingdom and be allowed to marry his daughter.

However, anyone who will try but fail will be put to death.

Many young men got themselves into trouble, assuming that they could fulfill this task.

But when it came to completing it, they went

from corner to corner and did not know where to start and where to finish, because not all flies make honey.

The king however kept his word and the would-be heroes were put to death.

During that time, there was a famous hero called Greuceanu.

Hearing, as everyone else, of the royal promise, he thought about it, then changed his mind, and then changed his mind once more.

Eventually, he decided to go for it, putting his faith in God's help and in his own bravery.

He set off to the royal court to put himself forward, yet a small part of him was still undecided whether to take on this difficult mission.

On his way he came across two men whom the king's servants were taking away to be put to death for deserting the king's army during a battle.

They were terrified, the poor men, but Greuceanu soothed them with words so sweet that they started to take heart.

Based on this happening, our hero decided on a plan of action.

"I will take on these men's cause," he said to himself. "If I succeed in persuading the king to withdraw the death warrant against these men, I will dare to take on this other task too. If not, I will take this as an omen and go back home. It is never a bad thing to attempt something."

And while thinking in this way, he arrived at the royal court.

When he came before the king, he put so much craft into his talk, and spoke so well, that the king decided he had unfairly sentenced the two men.

He took Greuceanu's advice that these men would be of better use as royal servants, and that he would be seen in a better light for showing mercy towards his people.

The men could barely contain their happiness when they heard they had been given a reprieve.

They thanked Greuceanu from the bottom of their hearts and promised that for the rest of their lives they will pray for his continued success.

Taking this as a good omen, Greuceanu went before the king for the second time.

"Almighty king," he said, "may you live many years on this enlightened throne of your kingdom. Many heroes have promised your Highness to take the sun and the moon back from the *zmei*, who have stolen them from the sky. I know these heroes have been put to death, because they have not been able to fulfill this promise they have made towards your Highness. I too, almighty king, would like to go in search of these thieving *zmei*, and to try my luck. Maybe God might enable me to punish those cursed *zmei* for their thoughtless daring. But I ask that you be merciful and helpful towards me."

"My dear Greuceanu," the king said, "I cannot change what I have previously decided, because I have to be fair. My commands will be the same for my entire kingdom. For me, favoritism is unlawful."

Seeing the king's determination and the fairness of his words, Greuceanu said:

"Let it be so, almighty king. I will not give up until I bring to good end the task I am taking upon myself of my own free will."

They agreed, and Greuceanu made all the preparations needed so he would come out of this endeavor safe and sound.

He took his brother with him and they went, and kept going, until they reached the Goldsmith-of-the-Earth's dwelling.

This Goldsmith-of-the-Earth was Greuceanu's blood brother.

He was the most skilled goldsmith across the entire earth, in addition to having magic powers.

For three days and three nights, Greuceanu and the goldsmith drew up a plan of action.

After that, Greuceanu and his brother went on their way.

As soon as Greuceanu left, the goldsmith began making the face of Greuceanu out of metal.

Then he asked his apprentices to keep it in the fire continuously day and night.

Meanwhile, Greauceanu and his brother walked a long way, and even longer, until they reached a crossroads.

Here they stopped, sat on the grass, and had a picnic using their food leftovers.

They decided to each take one of the two paths stretching out before them, to maximize their chances of finding the *zmei*.

Before going their separate ways, they tore a headscarf in two, each taking one half.

"As long as the headscarf will look worn along the edges," they said, "there is hope to meet one another safe and sound. But if the headscarf gets torn in the middle, the other one has died."

They also stuck a knife in the ground and said:

"The one who is first to return to this spot and finds the knife rusted shouldn't spend time waiting for the other, because he has died."

Then they parted, after hugging and crying like babies.

Greuceanu went towards the right and his brother went towards the left.

Greuceanu's brother walked for a long time without finding anything.

He therefore returned to the spot where they had parted, and finding the knife in good condition, he started waiting for his brother.

Meanwhile, Greuceanu went and kept going along a path which ended right in front of the houses of the *zmei*, around where the devil weans his children.

Upon reaching this spot, Greuceanu did three summersaults and turned into a pigeon, as the Goldsmith-of-the-Earth had taught him to do.

As a pigeon, Greuceanu flew up to a tree branch which was right in front of the houses of the *zmei*.

Upon seeing the pigeon, the eldest daughter came out into the yard to take a closer look.

She called out to her mother and younger sister to come and see the miracle, because birds did not fly as far as their dwelling place.

"That pigeon does not look like a good omen," the youngest daughter said. "The eyes do not look like those of a bird, but rather they look like the eyes of Greuceanu the Golden. Our time may be drawing to a close. From here on, may God have mercy on us."

It seems the *zmei* had already heard of Greuceanu's bravery.

Then the three *zmeu* women went back inside and started devising a plan of defense.

Greuceanu made three summersaults and turned into a fly, so he could make his way undetected into the house of the *zmei*.

There he hid into the crack of one of the beams that were holding up the roof and listened to their plans.

After he heard everything they said, he left the house, transformed back into a human, and set off towards the Green Forest.

Along the way, he hid underneath a bridge.

From what he had heard while eavesdropping on the three *zmeu* women, he knew that the male *zmei* had gone hunting in the Green Forest.

One of them was due to return towards evening, another was due back towards midnight, and the head of the clan towards morning.

While Greuceanu was waiting, the youngest *zmeu* was on his way back.

As the *zmeu*'s horse was about to go over the bridge, he started snorting and jumping backwards seven steps.

"May the wolves devour this horse's flesh!" the *zmeu* shouted. "I don't fear anything in this world other than Greuceanu the Golden. But even him, I could slay with one strike."

"Come hither, brave *zmeu*," Greuceanu said, as he came out from under the bridge, "let us cut ourselves in swords, or fight each other chest to chest."

"Let us fight each other chest to chest, because that's fairer," the *zmeu* said.

They approached one another and started fighting.

The *zmeu* grabbed Greuceanu and stuck him into the earth right up to his knees.

But Greuceanu grabbed the *zmeu* and stuck

him into the earth up to his neck, then cut off his head.

After he threw the *zmeu*'s corpse, and that of his horse, underneath the bridge, he got some rest.

In the middle of the night, the elder brother was about to cross the same bridge when his horse jumped seventeen steps backwards.

The *zmeu* said the same words as his brother had done, and Greuceanu answered him in the same way.

Coming out from under the bridge, he started fighting this *zmeu* as well.

The *zmeu* grabbed Greuceanu and pushed him into the earth right up to the chest.

But Greuceanu, jumping out quickly, grabbed the *zmeu*, pushed him to the ground and into the earth right up to the neck and beheaded him with his sword.

Throwing away the *zmeu*'s corpse and that of his horse under the bridge, just as he had done with his younger brother, he once again had a rest.

Towards dawn came the big *zmeu*, the father-in-law of the two *zmei* Greuceanu had already killed.

The big *zmeu* was in a bad mood, and his mood became even worse when he reached the bridge and his horse jumped seventy-seven steps backwards.

The *zmeu* was furious and roared:

"May the wolves devour the flesh of my horse. There is nobody I fear on this earth, other than Greuceanu the Golden. And that one as well, I can do away with easily."

Greuceanu came out from under the bridge and said:

"Well then, brave *zmeu*, come and do so. We can cut each other in swords, hit each other with spears, or fight one other chest to chest."

They started fighting.

They fought using swords until their swords broke.

They fought using spears until their spears broke.

Then they started fighting chest to chest.

They were fighting so hard the earth was shaking underneath them.

The *zmeu* squeezed Greuceanu once, but Greuceanu, anticipating what the *zmeu* was about to do, swelled himself up and tensed his veins and did not suffer any pain.

Then Greuceanu squeezed the *zmeu* as well, when the *zmeu* wasn't expecting it, and the *zmeu*'s bones cracked.

No one had ever seen a fight such as this one.

And they fought, and fought, until the afternoon, when they got tired.

A raven flew above their head, watching their fight.

"Bring me a beak-full of water," the *zmeu* said to the raven, "and I will feed you a young man's corpse along with his horse's.

"Bring me a beak-full of water," Greuceanu said, "and I will feed you three *zmeu* corpses, along with those of their horses."

So the raven brought Greuceanu a beak-full of water and quenched his thirst.

With his forces replenished, Greuceanu heaved the *zmeu* up in the air and then threw him to the ground.

He pushed him in down to his neck, put his foot on the *zmeu*'s head and held him like this.

"Tell me, cursed *zmeu*," he said, "where have you hidden the sun and the moon? Because there is no escape for you."

The *zmeu* was stalling, telling him all sorts, but Greuceanu said:

"Tell me or if not, I will still find them, and I will cut off your head as well."

The *zmeu*, still hoping to escape with his life if he tells him, said:

"I keep them locked up in the Green Forest, inside a cabin. The key is my right hand pinky.

As soon as Greuceanu heard this, he beheaded the *zmeu* and cut off the pinky on the *zmeu*'s right hand.

He gave all the corpses to the raven, as he had promised, then went to the cabin in the Green Forest, opened the door using the *zmeu*'s pinky, and found the sun and the moon.

He took the sun into his right hand and the moon into his left, threw them into the sky, and rejoiced at the light they cast upon the earth.

Upon seeing the sun and the moon back in the sky, the people rejoiced and praised God for having given Greuceanu the strength to win against the *zmei*.

As for Greuceanu, he set off on his way back to the king, happy that he had brought his task to a good end.

He found his brother back at the crossroads and they hugged.

They bought two horses that could run as fast as the wind and set off back to the king.

Along the way, they came upon a tree full of golden pears.

Greuceanu's brother said that it would be good if they could rest a little under the shadow of this pear tree, to give the horses a chance to catch their breath.

He also wanted to pick a few pears to allay their hunger.

Greuceanu, who had heard what the *zmeu* women had in store, agreed to take a rest.

However, he did not let his brother pick any of the pears, but said he will pick them himself.

Then he took out his sword and cut off the roots of the pear tree.

When, what do you think?

Blood and venom started flowing from the pear tree, and they could hear a voice saying:

"You have killed me, Greuceanu, the way you have killed my husband."

And nothing remained of that pear tree other than dust and cinders.

Greuceanu's brother was stunned, not knowing what to make of this.

The two brothers continued their journey, until they reached a beautiful garden with flowers and butterflies and a tiny stream with clear, cool water.

"Let's stop here for a little while," Greuceanu's brother said, "to rest our horses, while we drink some water and pick some flowers."

"Let's do so, brother," Greuceanu said, "if this garden has been planted by human hands and this stream has been left here by God."

Then, taking out his sword, he hit at the root of a flower that was particularly beautiful.

He also stabbed into the bottom of the stream.

But instead of water, thick dark blood started bubbling up to the surface, as well as from the flower's root, and the air became filled with a disgusting smell.

Only dust was left of the eldest *zmeu* daughter, who had transformed into the garden and the spring to poison Greuceanu and kill him.

Having escaped this terrible trap, they mounted their horses and went on their way, riding as fast as the wind.

When, what do you think?

The *zmeu* matriarch had started following

them, with one jaw touching the sky and the other touching the ground, intending to swallow Greuceanu.

And she had reason to be furious, because he had killed her entire family.

"Look behind you, brother," Greuceanu said, "and tell me what you see."

"I see a cloud coming after us like a tornado," his brother said.

They spurred on their horses, and Greuceanu once again asked his brother to look behind him.

The brother said that the cloud is approaching like a flame.

So they spurred on their horses once more, until they reached the Goldsmith-of-the-Earth's dwelling.

There, as soon as they dismounted, they locked themselves in the smithy, where the old *zmeu* woman could not enter.

If she had reached them, she would have annihilated them.

Not even a little bone would have remained.

Now however, she could not do anything against them, so she turned to trickery.

She asked Greuceanu to make a hole in the wall, so she could at least see his face.

Greuceanu pretended to take pity on her and made a hole in the wall.

But the Goldsmith-of-the-Earth was waiting with the metal cast he had made of Greuceanu's face, which had been burning in the fire for so long that sparks were flying from it.

When the *zmeu* woman put her mouth at the crack in the wall to suck Greuceanu in, the Goldsmith-of-the-Earth shoved the fiery metal cast into her throat.

She swallowed it and died on the spot.

Her corpse soon transformed itself into a mountain made of metal.

The Goldmith-of-the-Earth opened the door of the smithy, went outside and they celebrated their victory for three days and three nights.

The Goldsmith-of-the-Earth was particularly happy about the mountain made of metal and asked his apprentices to turn it into a carriage and three horses for Greuceanu.

After that was done, the Goldsmith-of-the-Earth breathed life into the metal horses.

Saying goodbye to the Goldsmith-of-the-Earth, Greuceanu got into the carriage with his brother and left towards the king to receive his reward.

On their way, they reached a crossroads, where they stopped and rested.

Then, Greuceanu un-harnessed one of the horses from the carriage and gave it to his brother, to tell the king that Greuceanu was on his way, having completed his task.

He stayed somewhat behind, advancing at slow pace and recovering his strength in anticipation of his meeting with the king.

On his way, he passed by a lame devil who was holding up travelers to give them grief.

The devil was too scared to confront Greuceanu directly, but he didn't want to leave him untouched by devilish nastiness.

He therefore took out the nail from the head of the back axis and threw it a long way behind the carriage.

"Hey there young man," the devil said to Greuceanu, "you have lost your nail, go and find it."

Greuceanu jumped out of the carriage but left his sword there by mistake.

And while he was looking for the nail, the devil stole his sword.

Then, going to the side of the road, he made three summersaults and turned into a large rock.

Greuceanu put the nail back at the head of the axis, got back in the carriage, and went on his way, without realizing that his sword was missing.

One of the king's traitorous advisers had promised his offspring to the devil, if he will help him marry the king's daughter.

The devil knew that without his sword, Greuceanu was unrecognizable.

So he told the traitorous adviser to go before the king and ask for his daughter's hand in marriage, saying that it was he who had retrieved the sun and the moon from the *zmei*.

The king believed him, because he trusted his adviser and could see the sun and the moon back in the sky.

He therefore started to get things organized for the wedding.

While everyone was getting ready for the royal wedding, Greuceanu's brother arrived with the news that Greuceanu was on his way.

The adviser, as soon as he heard, went to the king and said that the new arrival is a fraud and must be put behind bars.

The king listened to him and Greuceanu's brother was put into prison.

Then the adviser spent from dawn till dusk every day hurrying everyone so the wedding could take place quicker.

He thought that, once he gets married to the king's daughter, the matter will be over and Greuceanu's arrival will not change things.

The king, however, did not like his adviser's attempt to rush things, and was stalling the preparations.

Not long passed and Greuceanu arrived and went before the king, saying he had completed the task.

But as he did not have his sword, the king did not recognize him.

That's when Greuceanu realized that his sword was missing.

He remembered that he only saw the rock by the side of the road after he had found the nail and was returning to the carriage with it, and understood that he had been tricked.

"Enlightened king," he said, "everyone speaks of your fairness. Please, let me have some justice. You have waited a long time for this wedding to take place. Please wait only for a little while longer, and you will see the truth reveal itself before your eyes."

The king agreed to wait until Greuceanu returns, having started to wonder whether his adviser had been telling the truth.

Greuceanu got back in his carriage and returned on his way until he reached the rock by the side of the road, where the devil had taken out the nail from his carriage.

"Unworthy creature," he said, "give me the sword you have stolen from me, because if not, I will turn you to dust."

The rock did not budge.

Greuceanu made three summersaults and turned himself into a mace made entirely of lead.

Then he started hitting the rock so hard, the earth was shaking.

Every time he would hit, a piece would fly out of the rock.

And he kept hitting until he smashed the rock's top to pieces.

Then suddenly the rock started shaking and asking for forgiveness.

Yet the mace only started hitting harder, and it kept hitting until the rock turned to dust.

When nothing remained of the rock,

Greuceanu searched among the dust and found his sword.

He took it and without resting a single moment, he returned before the king.

"I am ready, almighty king," he said, "to show whoever is asking what Greuceanu can do. Let that shameless adviser come, who had tried to deceive you."

The king called for the adviser to be brought in.

The latter, when he saw Greuceanu with his sword and his brow furrowed, started trembling and asking for forgiveness, revealing how the devil had tempted him into deceiving the king.

After Greuceanu intervened on his behalf, the adviser received forgiveness from the king, but was ordered to leave the kingdom.

Greuceanu's brother was released from prison and the royal wedding was arranged, which was joyful and lasted three whole weeks.

And I got into a saddle and told you the story thus.

TRANSLATOR'S NOTE (GREUCEANU)

In translating and adapting this story, I have made one change that is worth mentioning, which was to fix a glaring plot hole relating to Greuceanu's sword.

In the original version, the devil gives the impostor the sword he had stolen from Greuceanu, which the impostor uses to persuade the king of his victory over the *zmei*.

However, Greuceanu then goes back to the devil (transformed into a stone) and retrieves his sword from the devil.

This is problematic, because it means the sword was in two places at once: with the devil, and with the impostor hero.

To remedy this problem, in my version, the

devil does not hand the sword over to the impostor hero, but simply advises him to claim that he was the one to free the sun and the moon from the hands of the *zmei*.

I made the choice that the devil be the one who held on to the sword, so Greuceanu could retrieve it from him.

As Greuceanu cannot be recognized without his sword, and as the king is likely to trust his own advisor, it was plausible that the impostor could persuade the king even without having the sword.

I would also like to provide an explanation of what a *zmeu* is.

The *zmeu* (plural *zmei*) is a monster-like creature that appears in many Romanian fairy tales, legends, and myths.

Because the *zmeu* appears so often in these stories, this creature is never described, presumably because the people listening to the tales had a common understanding of what a *zmeu* looks like.

However, it is worth pointing out that there is no formal consensus over what a *zmeu* looks like.

This lack of clear description is perhaps why the *zmeu* is so popular in Romanian fairy tales.

Its monster-like features can easily be adapted by the storyteller to take the shape of whatever is needed by the narrative.

Some depictions show the *zmeu* as more human-like, while in others the *zmeu* seems to share a stronger resemblance to dragons.

If you are curious, I suggest you type the word into Google Images and enjoy the many different representations you will find.

I decided to add a short yet somewhat vague description of the *zmeu* ('fearsome human-like creatures with magic powers') in my translated version.

My intention was to indicate to the reader that the word refers to a fantastic creature that is part of Romanian folklore, while at the same time not limiting the reader's imagination to my own mental image of a *zmeu*.

The *zmeu* shares many human features.

Based on what happens in the stories, we can tell that the *zmeu* has arms and legs, as well as the ability to ride a horse and use weapons.

On the other hand, the *zmeu* is often described as having a tail and being able to blow fire through their mouth, as well as being bigger and stronger than humans.

In some stories, such as in the case of *Greuceanu*, the *zmeu* also has other magical powers, such as being able to shapeshift, often as part of their plan to trap and defeat the hero.

In most cases, the *zmeu* is an evil, cunning creature that kidnaps a beautiful maiden and keeps her prisoner until she is rescued by the hero.

In the case of *Greuceanu*, the beautiful maiden is replaced by the sun and the moon.

The *zmeu* is often helped by his mother, who usually has a whole range of magic powers and chases after the hero or attempts to outwit him once her son has been defeated.

In *Greuceanu*, there are three male and three female *zmei*, so there is a more complex dynamic, but the eldest of the *zmeu* women serves the same function as the ultimate avenger.

Greuceanu includes many beloved tropes: stealing something bright and beautiful that has to be retrieved by the hero, the chase, and the many obstacles the hero has to overcome in order to succeed.

There is also the attempt by the mother of the *zmeu* to kill the hero through blowing fire on him, which seems to be the undoing of many of the *zmeu* mothers.

If you decide to read more of my translated stories of Petre Ispirescu's collection, you will no doubt see some of these *zmeu*-related tropes in action in a variety of different stories.

KING ALEODOR

There was, once upon a time, a king who had reached old age and did not have an heir.

He was longing to have a son of his own, but in vain.

Eventually, luck smiled upon him and he had a charming little boy, one which you'd see and not forget.

The king called him Aleodor.

When it was time for the boy to get baptized, he called the East, the West, the North, and the South, so all would share in his joy.

The feasts to celebrate the boy's baptism lasted for three days and three nights, and the guests rejoiced so much they remembered it until their dying days.

While growing up, the boy was becoming cleverer and more skilled day by day.

Not long passed and the king was close to death.

"Daddy's dearest," he told his son just before dying, "I am about to take my last breath. I can see that you will become a great man. And even dead, my bones will rejoice in their grave over your achievements. I don't have anything to teach you about taking over the reins of this kingdom, because with your skill, I know you will do well. One thing I will tell you: do not be tempted to hunt on that mountain over there. If you do, great sorrow will fall upon your head. That mountain is the property of Half-a-Man-Riding-Half-a-Lame-Rabbit, and whoever steps on his property does not escape unpunished."

After the king said this, he opened his mouth three times and his soul flew away.

His family and his people grieved for him a long time.

In the end, they had to bury him, and Aleodor became the new king.

Despite his youth, Aleodor put the matters of the kingdom in order like a grown man.

Everybody was happy with the way he was

ruling, and the people were proud of their new king.

In his spare time, Aleodor liked to go hunting.

He remembered what his father had told him, and was following his word religiously.

But one day, without knowing how, he mindlessly set foot onto the land of the ugly man.

He had barely taken ten steps to return to his own lands when he found himself face to face with him.

He wasn't scared about having stepped on the man's land, but he was annoyed that he had gone against his father's dying words.

"All the lawless who step on my land become my slaves," the man said to him.

"First of all you should know," Aleodor responded, "that I did it out of mindlessness and without intention. I do not harbor any negative thoughts against you."

"I thought you'd be different," the ugly man said. "But I see that you intend to ask forgiveness from me, like all the other cowards."

"On the contrary, God forbid! I have told you the naked truth. If you want a fight, choose your weapon: we can cut each other with swords, hit each other with a mace, or we can fight with our bare hands."

"None of these will do. There is no other way to escape punishment than to bring me the daughter of the Green King, so I can marry her."

Aleodor attempted to avoid the challenge.

He said that the affairs of his kingdom do not permit him to take such a long trip, nor does he have a guide to find his way to the Green King.

He tried one argument after another, but in vain.

The ugly man didn't care about any of these things.

He kept on and on that he wanted Aleodor to bring him the daughter of the Green King.

Otherwise, Aleodor will receive the punishment dished out to thieves for mistreating other people's rights.

Aleodor knew he was guilty.

Even though it had been unintentional, he knew he had done wrong in stepping on the ugly man's property.

He also knew that there is no point to argue with the man of the devil.

In the end, he promised to fulfill the task he had been asked to do.

Half-a-Man-Riding-Half-a-Lame-Rabbit knew that, because Aleodor had promised, he will keep his word, because he was that sort of man.

"Go with God," he told Aleodor, "and may you return having fulfilled the task."

Aleodor set off on his quest.

On his way, while thinking how best to fulfill the task, he found himself at the edges of a swamp.

He saw a pike fighting for her life on dry land and was about to catch the pike to make himself something to eat.

"Don't kill me, King Aleodor," the pike said. "Better put me back into the water, and I will come to your help when you'll need it."

Aleodor put her back in the water.

"Take this scale," the pike said. "When you'll think of me, I will come to your aid."

Aleodor went on his way, dazed by all that had happened to him that day.

Suddenly, he came across a raven that had a broken wing.

Just when he was about to catch the raven for his dinner, the raven spoke.

"Instead of burdening your soul with my

death," the raven said, "better bandage up my wing, and I will do much good to you one day."

Aleodor agreed and bandaged up the raven's wing.

When he was about to go, the raven said:

"Take this feather, brave lad, and when you'll think of me, I will come to your aid."

Aleodor took the feather and went on his way.

He had barely taken a few steps when he came across a gadfly.

Just as he was preparing to crush it with his foot, the gadfly spoke.

"Spare my life, King Aleodor," the gadfly said, "and I will save your life one day. Take this little bit of fluff from my wing, and when you think of me, I will come to your aid."

Hearing the gadfly speak, Aleodor lifted his foot and took the gadly's bit of fluff.

After walking for I don't know how many days, he reached the palace of the Green King.

Aleodor went to the gate and waited for someone to come and ask him what he was looking for.

He waited for one day, then a second day.

On the third day, the Green King called his

servants and gave them a telling off to be remembered.

"Why is it," he said, "that someone has been standing by the gate for three days and no one has gone to find out what he wants? Is this what I am paying you for?"

The servants were floundering and did not know what to say.

In the end, they opened the gate and brought Aleodor before the king.

"What is it you want, young lad?" asked the king.

"Great king," Aleodor answered, "I have been sent to ask for your daughter's hand in marriage."

"Fine, my lad. But first we have to make an agreement, because this is the custom in my kingdom. You are allowed to hide wherever you may want every day, for three consecutive days. If my daughter finds you each time you hide, your head will be cut off and will be put on the stilt that has remained, from one hundred, without a head. If you manage to remain hidden from her even once during these three days, you can take her from me with my blessing."

"I trust that God will not let me die," Aleodor

said. "We can give the stilt something other than a human head. I am happy to enter into this agreement."

"Is that so?"

"It is."

They made the agreement legally binding.

As soon as the agreement was made, Aleodor started thinking and rethinking how best to hide from the Green King's daughter.

And while thinking and planning, he remembered the pike.

He took out the scale, looked at it, and thought of its owner.

Suddenly, the pike was by his side.

"What is it you want, King Aleodor?"

The boy told the pike about his predicament and asked for help.

"Don't worry. Leave it to me," said the pike.

She gave one swish of her tail and transformed Aleodor into a little fish, which she hid at the bottom of the sea, among the other little fish.

When the girl woke up, she looked through her magic looking glass, which she had used to find all her suitors up until this point, but she could not see him.

The girl was delighted to finally come across

a young man who was presenting her with a challenge.

While the others who had come to ask for her hand had hidden in cellars, behind houses, or behind a stack of hay, Aleodor had hidden himself in such a way that the girl started to worry she might get beaten at her own game.

But just then she got the idea to point her looking glass at the sea, and she soon found him hiding among the little fish.

"Get out of there, you thief," she told him laughing. "From a normal-sized human being you have transformed yourself into a little fish and have hidden at the bottom of the sea."

He didn't have a choice and had to come out.

She told the king:

"I think, father, that with this lad I have found my match. He is handsome and cute too, and not dumb like the others. He looks like he's of a special kind."

"We shall see," the king said.

The next day, Aleodor thought of the raven, who immediately appeared before him.

"What do you want, master?" the raven asked.

Aleodor told him about his predicament and asked the raven for help.

The raven agreed.

With a swish of his wing, the raven transformed Aleodor into a raven chick and hid him in a raven's nest that had been swept up into the air by a gale of wind.

As soon as the girl woke up, she looked through her looking glass, but couldn't find him anywhere.

She searched for him all over the earth, but he wasn't there.

She searched for him through the seas and oceans, he wasn't there either.

The girl was dumbfounded.

Then she suddenly had an idea and used her looking glass to search the skies.

She found him in the heights of the skies among the other raven chicks and wagged her finger at him.

"Come back down, you thief!" she said. "You're not a raven chick. But I appreciate the irony of trying to escape by ascending to heaven."

Aleodor did not have a choice and came back down to earth.

The king started to marvel at Aleodor's cleverness and wondered whether his daughter may indeed have found her match.

"Let's see where he will hide this time," the king said.

On the third day, early in the morning, Aleodor thought of the gadfly.

She came as soon as he held her wing fluff.

After Aleodor told her why he needed help, the gadfly said:

"Leave it to me, I promise she won't be able to find you."

She transformed him into a louse and hid him in the girl's hair.

When the girl woke up and took her looking glass, she searched for him all day long, but could not find him.

She was at her wit's end.

She used her looking glass to search through the seas, all over the earth, and through the whole of the sky, yet she couldn't find him anywhere.

Towards evening, tired of so much searching, she admitted defeat.

"Show yourself. I can sense that you are close by, but I cannot see you. You have beaten me, I will be yours."

Once he heard that she had admitted defeat,

Aleodor climbed down from her hair and showed himself.

The king had no option but to allow Aleodor to take the girl with him.

They left in style, with crowds accompanying them right up to the edges of the kingdom.

On the way, they stopped for a rest.

After they ate this and that, Aleodor put his head in the girl's lap and fell asleep.

The king's daughter, looking at him, could not get over how handsome he was.

Her heart gave a jolt and she kissed him.

Aleodor woke up with a start and jumped several feet away from her, horrified.

"You cannot kiss me, it is forbidden," he said. "I have not taken you for myself, but for the one who has sent me."

"Why did you not tell me?" she said. "I would have known what to do. But the time is not yet lost."

They set off and arrived on the lands of Half-a-Man-Riding-Half-a-Lame-Rabbit.

"I have accomplished the task," Aleodor said, "and I will now take my leave."

The girl, when she saw Half-a-Man-Riding-Half-a-Lame-Rabbit, shook with disgust.

The horrible man stood close to the girl and started flattering her, trying to sweeten her up.

"Disappear from my sight, devil," the girl told him, "because I will send you to your mother, Hell, which has spilt you upon this earth."

The horrible man was lying on his belly, pleading with the girl to take him as a husband, but in vain.

He could not even come near her, because she would hold him away with her eyes.

She did not call him other than devil and disgustingness.

"Disappear, unclean one, from the face of the earth, so the world can get rid of a plague like you."

He kept trying for a while, but when he saw how strongly she was resisting his advances, he burst from anger, for having been made a laughing stock by a woman.

Aleodor married the girl.

Then he stretched out his lands to include those of Half-a-Man-Riding-Half-a-Lame-Rabbit and took his wife back to his own kingdom.

When the crowds saw him returning safely, they were overcome with joy.

They were also delighted when they met his

wife, who was so beautiful that she made even the stars smile.

The young couple reigned and lived happily, until the day they died.

And I got into a saddle and told you the story thus.

TRANSLATOR'S NOTE (KING ALEODOR)

The girl in this fairy tale is one of the most delightful female heroines I have encountered throughout Petre Ispirescu's collection.

She is in charge of her destiny, she has magic powers, and she knows what she wants.

Above all, she is mischievous, and loves a challenge.

Despite the deadly danger that Aleodor is in, if he fails at his task, her responses to his attempts lighten the mood.

This heroine's agency stands in stark contrast to Greuceanu's bride in the previous story, who does not even feature as a character and seems to be a pawn in the game played by the various male characters.

Nevertheless, I decided to make one change in my translated version of *King Aleodor* that pertains to the girl.

In the original version, when she kisses Aleodor and he wakes up, he slaps her.

I decided to replace the slap with him jumping out of his slumber.

It is clear from the way his slap is described in the original version that slapping her for kissing him is perceived as noble, a sign of his integrity.

He slaps her because he wants to keep his word to Half-a-Man-Riding-Half-a-Lame-Rabbit and does not want to fall into temptation.

However, from our 21st century perspective, slapping a woman is a horrifying act of violence, and would not provide the foundation for a blossoming romance.

Interestingly, given the girl's character, it is unlikely that such an emancipated and strong woman would have tolerated being slapped, regardless of reasons.

As such, I feel the change I have made is more in keeping with her character, and therefore is an improvement on the original version of the story.

THE MAGIC WOLF

There was once a king and queen who had three sons.

They also had a very beautiful garden.

The king liked this garden so much, that he was tending to it himself.

At the bottom of the garden, an apple tree had grown which was entirely made of gold.

The king was overcome with happiness that in his garden there was an apple tree unlike any other tree in the whole wide world.

He kept going to it and looking at it from all sides.

One day, he was delighted to see the tree budding, going into bloom, the flowers falling, and the fruit starting to show.

Then, towards the evening, the fruit started ripening.

The king was smiling from ear to ear.

He was salivating at the thought that the next day, he would be able to have at his table golden apples, something hitherto unheard of.

Early the next morning, the king went into the garden to pick some golden apples and find out how they tasted.

But the tree did not have any ripe fruit hanging from it.

It was as if the fruit that had started to show the previous day had vanished without trace.

But while the king was standing there, staring at the tree that had given him so much hope the previous day, he saw some buds appearing and going into bloom.

Then he saw the flowers fall and the fruit starting to show again.

At the promise of another opportunity to sample the golden apples, the king recovered from his disappointment and was happy to wait until the next day.

However, the next day, once again, the tree was devoid of apples.

The king was extremely cross and ordered

his guards to catch the thieves, but night after night, the guards failed to do so.

The tree was going into bloom every day, the flowers would fall off, the fruit would grow and by the evening, the apples would start to ripen.

Who was coming at night and taking the apples, without the king's people finding out?

It looked like whoever it was, they were doing it to spite the king and his guards.

The king was so upset by this that he was willing to relinquish his throne and leave it to whomever would be able to catch the thief.

The king's eldest son came before him and asked for permission to guard the tree.

The king greeted his eldest son's request with great enthusiasm and the young man set to work.

He kept watch that night, but the same thing happened as to the guards who had kept watch before him: he fell asleep, and by the morning, the fruit were gone once again.

The following night, the middle son kept watch.

He had no more success than his elder brother, and returned to his father not having accomplished anything.

They both said that they had succeeded in

staying awake until midnight, but afterwards they could not keep their eyes open any more and fell into a deep sleep, unaware of anything that was going on around them.

The youngest son was listening and keeping quiet.

Then, after his brothers finished telling their father what had happened, he asked his father to let him keep watch as well.

As sad as the king was that neither of his two older sons had been able to catch the apple thief, he laughed when he heard his youngest son's request.

But after many pleas, he allowed him to stand guard for one night.

As soon as evening came, the youngest son took his quiver of arrows, his bow, and his sword, and went into the garden.

He found himself a solitary spot, far removed from any of the trees and fences, so he wouldn't have anything to lean on.

Instead, he decided to remain standing on the stump of a cut-down tree.

That way, when sleep would come upon him and he would start getting drowsy, he would fall down and wake up.

Indeed, after falling down a couple of times, his sleepiness went away and he remained awake and unplagued by the temptation to sleep.

Towards daybreak, when the sleep is sweetest, he heard a rustling.

It seemed to be coming from a flock of birds that was flying towards the tree.

As he kept listening, he soon heard someone plundering the apple tree.

He took out an arrow from his quiver, put it against his bow, and released it in the general direction where the rustling was coming from.

There was no movement.

He released another arrow and once again, nothing.

When he released the third, the rustling could be heard again and he understood that the flock of birds must have flown away.

He approached the apple tree and saw that the thieves hadn't had time to take all the apples.

They had taken some, but there were still apples left hanging from the tree.

While he was examining the area, he saw something shiny on the ground.

He bent down and picked up the shiny

object, and saw it was a feather made entirely of gold.

He picked a few apples, put them on a golden platter, and with the feather in his cap he went before his father.

The king was ecstatic when he saw the apples.

He started spreading the news through his entire kingdom that his youngest son had succeeded in bringing him golden apples and finding out that the thief was a bird.

The boy asked his father for permission to go after the thief, but the king was no longer interested in pursuing that mission.

He was satisfied with having been able to see and taste the golden apples.

However, the boy did not leave it at that and eventually persuaded his father to allow him to go on a quest to catch the thief.

To prepare for the road, he took clothes to wear, money to spend, and asked his most loyal servant to accompany him.

Then, with the quiver of arrows on his back and a sword hanging from his left thigh, the king's youngest son and his servant set off on their quest.

They went, and kept going, until they reached the desert.

Here they had some rest and decided to go towards the East.

Still travelling for a good long while, they reached a big forest that was rich and thick.

While making their way through the undergrowth, they saw in the distance a big wolf with a copper forehead and prepared themselves for defense.

The boy took an arrow out of his quiver, ready to strike.

"Wait, Prince Charming," the wolf shouted, "don't release your arrow. I will do much good to you one day".

The boy listened to the wolf and did not release his arrow.

The wolf asked the boy where he was going and what he was hoping to find in those woods untouched by human foot.

The boy told him about the the apples in his father's garden and that he was on his way to catch the thief.

The wolf said that the apples had been stolen by the king of the birds.

This bird had gathered his most agile

companions to be part of his flock, and they had flown together to steal the apples.

The wolf also told the boy that this bird belonged to a king whose kingdom was located at the edge of the forest and showed him the easiest way to reach that kingdom.

Then, giving him a small pretty apple, the wolf said:

"When you will need my help, look at this apple, think of me, and I will immediately appear by your side."

The boy took the apple and put it close to his chest.

Then, saying good-bye, he took off accompanied by his faithful servant.

They went through the thick of the forest and reached the kingdom the wolf had directed them towards.

They started speaking to inhabitants of that kingdom and were told that the king was keeping the bird in a golden cage in his garden.

That is all they needed to know.

They circled the royal courtyard a few times and noted all the details that seemed relevant.

As evening fell, they hid close to the wall

surrounding the courtyard and waited until everybody had gone to sleep.

Then, the servant kept watch as the boy climbed onto the edge of the wall and jumped into the courtyard.

He soon located the bird, but when he grabbed the cage, the bird gave out an ear-splitting shriek.

The boy immediately found himself surrounded by a multitude of birds, some big, some small, all shrieking in their own language.

They made such noise that the king's servants woke up.

When they went into the garden to investigate, they found the boy holding the cage and defending himself while the birds were trying to tear him to pieces.

The servants grabbed the boy and brought him before the king, who had also woken up and wanted to know what was happening.

As soon as the king saw the boy, he knew who he was.

"I am sorry, Prince Charming, that this has happened," the king said. "If you had come to me in good faith to ask for the bird, I might have been persuaded to give it to you willingly. But now, as you have been caught red-handed, you have to be put to death, as this is our custom. And your name will be sullied with the label of thief."

"This bird, enlightened king," the boy said, "has plundered us repeatedly of the golden apples that my father has in his garden. This is why I have come, to catch the thief."

"There might be truth in what you say, Prince Charming, but I cannot go against our customs. Only a significant deed of bravery done for the benefit of our kingdom can rescue you from the death penalty."

"Tell me what task to accomplish, and I will take it on."

"If you will bring me the white mare which is at the court of the neighboring king, you will escape unpunished, and I will give you the bird."

The boy took on the task, and he left that same day with his servant.

When they reached the court of the neighboring king, they spent some time finding out about the mare and the royal court.

Then, as evening came, the boy found a spot close to the wall surrounding the palace courtyard, from where they could observe what was going on inside the yard.

They watched as two servants took the mare for a walk, and marveled at her beauty.

She had a golden bridle decorated with precious stones that shone brighter than the sun.

Towards midnight, when the sleep is at its sweetest, the boy told his servant to keep watch while he climbed onto the wall and jumped into the king's courtyard.

He went on the tips of his toes until he reached the stables.

There he opened the door, grabbed the bridle, and pulled the mare towards him.

Everything was going smoothly until the mare reached the doors of the stables and neighed so loudly that the skies started screaming.

Her neighing was heard throughout the entire royal palace and woke up the king's servants, who immediately rushed to the stables to find out what was happening.

They grabbed the boy and took him before the king, who had also woken up.

As soon as the king saw the boy, he knew

who he was, and confronted him about the cowardly deed he was about to commit.

As the previous king had done, he told the boy that the custom of his country was to put thieves to death, and he did not have the power to overturn these customs.

The boy told him the entire story with the apples, the bird, and what the neighboring king had asked him to do.

Then the king said:

"If you bring me the Fair Maiden, you will escape death and your name will remain untarnished."

The boy took on the challenge and set off, accompanied by his servant.

On the way he remembered the little apple the wolf had given him.

He took it out, looked at it, and thought of the wolf, who immediately appeared before him.

"What is your wish, Prince Charming?" the wolf asked.

The boy told him everything that had happened and asked the wolf how to accomplish the latest task.

"It's an easy one," the wolf said. "Leave things to me, it's as good as done."

And the three of them set off towards the Fair Maiden.

When they got close to the Fair Maiden's dwelling, they took a rest in a forest from which the Maiden's bright palace could be seen.

And how beautiful the Fair Maiden's palace was.

Even the wolf marveled at its order and symmetry.

The next morning, they agreed that the boy and his servant would wait for the wolf by the trunk of an old tree.

As soon as the wolf arrived at the Fair Maiden's palace, he found a way to sneak into the garden.

He noticed that the leaves of the trees had all fallen off, so they were entirely bare, even though it wasn't winter.

On the ground, the fallen leaves were dry and brittle.

Only one rose bush still had its leaves and was full of buds, some in bloom and others open.

In order to reach it, the wolf had to walk on the tips of his toes so as not to rustle the dry leaves, and hid in that flowery bush.

While the wolf waited and kept watch, the

Fair Maiden came out of her palace accompanied by twenty-four servants, and she started to walk through the garden.

When the wolf saw her, he was so astounded by her beauty that he was on the point of inadvertently revealing himself, but he managed to regain his control just in time.

Her hair was entirely golden, arranged in braids that were long and thick.

When she was looking at someone with her big black eyes, she could make that person sick with longing.

Her eyebrows were well-arched, as if they had been painted on, and her skin was whiter than milk foam.

After walking through the garden a few times followed by her servants, she went to the rose bush to pick a few flowers.

The wolf jumped out of the rose bush, took her in his arms, and ran towards the spot where the boy was waiting while her servants dispersed in fright.

The Fair Maiden fainted from the shock, so the wolf placed her into the boy's arms.

The boy was mesmerized by her beauty, and fell in love with her straight away.

When the Fair Maiden woke up, she took one look at him and fell in love with him as well.

They decided that they did not want to part from one another, and told each other their life story.

"Leave it to me," the wolf said, when he saw the love that had blossomed between them. "I can make things turn out as you wish."

On their way to the king who had asked the boy to bring him the Fair Maiden, the wolf made three summersaults and transformed into the exact likeness of the Fair Maiden.

They agreed that the boy's servant would stay with the Fair Maiden by the root of a big tree in the forest, until the boy returns with the white mare.

When he reached the king's court, the boy handed over the wolf, disguised as the Fair Maiden.

As soon as the king saw her, his heart melted and an untold longing took hold of him.

The king said:

"Your bravery, Prince Charming, has rescued you from death and a bad reputation. Now I will reward you for it by giving you the mare."

As soon as the boy took hold of the mare's bridle, he went on his way.

The real Fair Maiden climbed on the mare, and they rode over the borders of this kingdom.

Meanwhile, the king gathered his advisers and went to the church to marry the Fair Maiden.

When he reached the door of the church, the wolf did three summersaults, turned back into a wolf, and fletched his fangs at the king's guards.

When they saw the wolf with his enormous fangs, the guards froze in fear.

Then, after they found their bearings, they tried to chase after the wolf with boos and shouts.

But the wolf fastened his pace until he could no longer be seen in the distance.

By using shortcuts, he soon caught up with the boy and accompanied him on his way to the king who had asked for the mare.

When they got close to the royal palace, they did as they had with the previous king.

The wolf transformed into the white mare, and the boy handed him over.

The king was overjoyed to see the mare.

After he welcomed the boy with great honor, the king said:

"Well done, Prince Charming, you have escaped both death as well as a bad reputation. I will hold my royal promise and will always be grateful to you."

He handed over the bird to the boy, who took the birdcage in which the bird was kept, said his goodbyes, and left.

He reached the forest where the Fair Maiden, the mare, and his servant were waiting, and they set off together to his father's kingdom.

The king who had received the mare ordered his entire army and his most high-ranking aristocrats to come out into the field.

He wanted to show them how well he could ride that most famous mare.

When the soldiers saw him, they all shouted:

"Live long, king, for having acquired such a treasure. May your mare, which you are riding so skillfully, live many years."

And indeed, the mare galloped, with the king on top, as if it was flying, its hooves barely touching the ground.

They started a competition.

But no one came anywhere close to catching up with the mare, because she left every other horse behind.

Once the wolf, disguised as the mare, had gathered a good distance, he suddenly stopped, threw the king off his back, made three summersaults, and transformed back into a wolf.

Then he ran, and ran, and kept running, until he reached the boy.

When they were about to part, the wolf said to the boy:

"This time, all your wishes have come true. But for the rest of your life, refrain from wishing for things that are beyond your abilities."

Then they parted, each going their own way.

When the boy and the Fair Maiden reached the kingdom belonging to the boy's father, people welcomed them, young and old.

They greatly rejoiced when they saw the Fair Maiden, who looked more beautiful than any other woman on earth.

As soon as he arrived, the boy ordered a beautiful stable to be made for the mare, and he placed the cage with the bird on the windowsill facing the garden.

Then his father started organizing everything for the wedding, and after a few days, the boy and the Fair Maiden got married.

The table was spread for all the guests, and the festivities lasted three days and three nights.

After that they lived happily ever after, because the boy had nothing left to wish for.

They may still be alive today, if they haven't yet died.

And I got into a saddle and told you the story thus.

TRANSLATOR'S NOTE (THE MAGIC WOLF)

One of the aspects I find so enjoyable about the fairy tales in Petre Ispirescu's collection is that many of them have a raw, unpolished quality that provides a rich source of inspiration for creativity.

This tale is one such story, with many of the elements barely sketched out, which seems to invite the reader into a collaborative imaginative exercise to fill in the missing pieces.

For instance, similarly to *King Aleodor*, the hero in this story also receives magical help from an animal as a result of a good deed, a common trope in fairy tales.

But the magical helper element is not as well

developed as in the *King Aleodor* story, where that element is fully explored.

The wolf in this tale could be more richly drawn out, and his relationship to the hero explored in more detail, but all this is left to the reader's imagination.

There is a farcical feel to the wolf's actions, especially when the wolf reveals his identity to the two kings who have been duped by his shapeshifting abilities.

For creative people looking for inspiration, this mixture of humorous and magical elements could become a rich source of raw story seeds.

The love story between the hero and the Fair Maiden is also not explored in any depth, but the small details that are provided, such as the barren courtyard with only one blooming rosebush, offer a myriad of creative possibilities.

At the end of the story, *The Magic Wolf* delivers a message that is popular in Romanian literature: do not stretch your luck by wishing for things beyond your abilities.

If you would like to read a story that explores this message in more depth, I recommend the novel *Moara cu Noroc* by Ioan Slavici, which has been translated into English as *The Lucky Mill*.

As you have been reading this story, you may have wondered about the use of the title 'Prince Charming', which appears several times in this story.

The original version of this title is 'Fat Frumos', which is a name often given to the male hero in Romanian fairy tales.

A literal translation might be 'Handsome Youth' or 'Lad Handsome' (*frumos* means 'handsome' and *fat* refers to a young man).

I chose to translate this title as 'Prince Charming' as this is a well-known way to refer to a male hero in the English language.

I would like to ask you for a small favor.

Reviews are the best way to spread the word about this book.

If you have enjoyed reading this book, it would mean a lot to me if you could leave a review.

Even if you only write a sentence or two, it will help. Thank you!

ABOUT THE AUTHOR

Petre Ispirescu was born in 1830 in Bucharest, where he lived most of his life. He grew up around folk stories, and was greatly inspired by them.

His parents wanted him to become a priest, a career path that required him to start training since childhood.

But at age 14, Ispirescu dropped out of his priest training and took up an apprenticeship at a publishing house.

He was a hard worker and quickly rose through the ranks.

Eventually, he was able to publish his own projects, which is how his collection of fairy tales came about.

He started publishing fairy tales as early as 1862 and continued publishing them over the following two decades.

Sadly, Petre Ispirescu died from a stroke at age 57.

Yet a few of the fairy tales he collected and published are still part of the Romanian literature curriculum to this day.

ABOUT THE TRANSLATOR

Alexa Ispas grew up in Romania and moved to Scotland at age 18.

She holds a PhD in psychology from the University of Edinburgh.

Her frequent visits to the Scottish Storytelling Centre inspired her to delve into her Romanian story heritage.

These explorations led her to discover old, forgotten Romanian gems that give us a glimpse into a way of life different from our own.

You can find more of Alexa's translations of old Romanian stories at www.storybothy.com

GET A FREE STORY

Jack the Pimple

Can the ugliest boy in the village marry the beautiful princess?

Read this charming story from 19th century Romania, collected by Petre Ispirescu and translated into English by Alexa J Ispas.

Download for free when you sign up to the newsletter at

www.storybothy.com/newsletter

Made in the USA
Monee, IL
02 December 2023